Dragonfly Magic

by

JM Sheridan

To Emily,
light up the world
with the magic
inside of you –

JM Sh

AuthorHouse™
1663 Liberty Drive
Bloomington, IN 47403
www.authorhouse.com
Phone: 1 (800) 839-8640

Published by AuthorHouse 11/13/2015

ISBN: 978-1-5049-6238-4 (sc)
978-1-5049-6240-7 (e)

Library of Congress Control Number: 2015918924

Print information available on the last page.

Any people depicted in stock imagery provided by Thinkstock are models,
and such images are being used for illustrative purposes only.
Certain stock imagery © Thinkstock.

This book is printed on acid-free paper.

authorHOUSE®

This book is dedicated to my loving family, Kevin and Brianna. To Kevin for all of his support and encouragement and for believing in me every step of the way; I love you so much. To Brianna, you are my inspiration, you are my muse, you are the beat of my heart. You fill my world with vibrant color.

To all of my friends who spread the word and help support me, a very heartfelt thank you.

To Chelsey for your keen proofreading skills!

To Janey for her beautiful poetry. Keep strong.

And to Cecilia, thank you for the lovely illustrations! Youngatheartstudios.com

Make a wish...

The Best Kind of Magic

Be very still
Don't make a sound
Lift your eyes to the sky
then back to the ground
Put your fingers in the grass
turn your face to the breeze
There's magic in the wings
of dragonflies and bees
A dandelion blows
a thousand kisses
And sprinkles the earth
with unlimited wishes
The stars all twinkle
their endless light
And the moon smiles down
on us every night
But the best kind of magic
lives inside our soul
It's the kind we take with us
wherever we go

by
Janey Coyne-Scaturro
Published on Amazon and Facebook

Brianna smiled as she looked at her reflection in the big mirror on the wall. "Don't I look just like a fairy?" she asked the little black-and-white cow on her bed. "I'll bet I can find lots of magic now, Mrs. Moomoo," Brianna said as she pushed her blue-rimmed eyeglasses back into place. Brianna looked around her room with an inquisitive eye. *Do any of my things have magic?* she wondered.

Brianna tucked Mrs. Moomoo into the pocket of her dress and headed for the toy box. She pulled out all kinds of dolls, blocks, crayons, and coloring books. She even pulled out one of Billy the cat's toys. Brianna inspected each item with a sniff and a shake and a tug, but nothing appeared to have magic. "Aw pickle sticks," she said and tossed the squeaky toy aside. "C'mon, Mrs. Moomoo," Brianna said as with determination. "Let's go find some magic!"

Brianna grabbed her sparkly blue sneakers and headed down to the kitchen, where her mother was making breakfast. She watched her mother flip each pancake with care so it would not break apart. Her tummy began to grumble. Brianna knew that once the pancakes were flipped, it was almost time to eat.

She climbed up onto her favorite chair, and put her magic wand and Mrs. Moomoo on the kitchen table beside her. Brianna began putting on her shoes one at a time. Left foot first and then the right foot. She noticed that her blue shoes were almost as sparkly as her magic wand. "Are shoes magic, Mama?" she asked as she pushed her eyeglasses back into place.

"No, Brianna," her mother answered bending down to help her tie her shoes. "Shoes are just shoes, and shoes are not magic."

As her mother put a plate of steaming pancakes in front of her, Brianna's mouth began to water. The smell of melted butter and syrup made its way down to her belly. "What about pancakes, Mama?" Brianna asked. "Pancakes taste so good; they must be magic," Brianna said and stuffed a big piece into her mouth, after offering a bite to Mrs. Moomoo.

"No, Brianna," her mother answered, drying her hands on a towel and smiling over her shoulder. "Pancakes are just pancakes, and pancakes are not magic."

"Aw pickle sticks," Brianna said with subtle disappointment. "Don't give up yet, Mrs. Moomoo." She said as she glanced at her friend."

"After breakfast, we can go outside to play," her mother said. "The sun is shining, and it looks like a beautiful day to make a sandcastle."

Good idea, Brianna thought. *I am sure to find magic outside.*

Brianna finished her breakfast and helped her mother clean up the dishes. Afterward, she grabbed Mrs. Moomoo and her magic wand and headed outside on her quest to find magic.

As Brianna made her way across the yard to the sandbox, Billy the cat walked over and rubbed against her legs. His purr was loud and happy as his tail swept around her knees. She knelt down on the soft grass and scratched Billy under his chin. His face was mostly white, but his big body had so many colors that it looked like one of Brianna's finger paintings. "Is ... Billy ... magic, Mama?" Brianna grunted as she attempted to heft Billy up off the ground.

"No, Brianna," her mother answered and reached to give Billy a pat between his ears. "Billy is just a cat, and cats are not magic."

"Aw pickle sticks," Brianna sighed as she released her hold on Billy. She tugged Mrs. Moomoo from her pocket. "Don't give up yet, Mrs. Moomoo. We will find magic; I just know we will!"

Brianna's face and head began to prickle from the warm sun in the sky. Her nose tingled with the smells of fresh cut grass and blooming flowers. She watched the bees busy at work in the garden as they traveled from flower to flower. She also heard the cicadas' as they loudly played their summer song in the maple trees.

While Mrs. Moomoo, Brianna, and her mom began constructing their sandcastle, a dragonfly landed on the edge of the sandbox. The insect had a small body with a very long tail and patterned wings. *It looks like a magic wand,* Brianna thought, *it must be magic.*

"Are dragonflies magic, Mama?" Brianna asked repositioning her eyeglasses.

"No, Brianna," her mother answered as she filled a bucket with play sand. "Dragonflies are just dragonflies, and dragonflies are not magic."

"Aw pickle sticks," Brianna said as she and Mrs. Moomoo moved closer to inspect the bug.

Brianna and Mrs. Moomoo were just inches away from the dragonfly when it sprang off the sandbox and into the air. Startled, Brianna fell backward and landed right on top of her sandcastle.

"Aw pickle sticks," Brianna said as she looked down at her flattened castle. "Looks like we have to start all over, Mrs. Moomoo."

Brianna set Mrs. Moomoo on the edge of the turtle sandbox and started to rebuild her castle. As she scooped and patted, dug and shaped, it wasn't long before her castle was rebuilt. "Done!" she exclaimed as she stood up to admire her hard work. "What do you think of our castle?"

When Brianna turned to pick up Mrs. Moomoo, she saw a dragonfly on top of the little cow's head. Brianna gasped and crouched down slowly. "Don't move Mrs. Moomoo," she whispered. "A dragonfly is on your head!"

As Brianna extended her fingers to touch the dragonfly, it popped off Mrs. Moomoo and flew over to the rose garden. Her eyes grew wide with excitement as she noticed three other dragonflies in the garden as well. Turning back around towards her mother, she observed dozens of dragonflies moving about the yard.

Brianna grabbed Mrs. Moomoo and gave her eyeglasses a little tap, then scurried to each dragonfly, trying to touch it. But the dragonflies were too quick, zooming into the air and just out of her reach. They darted up and down, forward and back, as if they were dancing around her. Brianna laughed and laughed as she and Mrs. Moomoo bounded across the yard, hoping to catch at least one dragonfly.

Tired and breathless, Brianna returned to her mother and their sandcastle. As she reached for her bucket, a large dragonfly landed on her hand. The insect was blue with black spots and had a very long tail. Its big, colorful wings sparkled in the sun, and its shimmering eyes were as big as Mrs. Moomoo's eyes. Brianna felt a tickle as its legs moved across her skin. She wondered how the insect's spindly little legs could possibly hold up such a big body.

Brianna leaned in nose-to-nose with the dragonfly. Suddenly it sprang off her hand and began to whiz around her. She grabbed Mrs. Moomoo and squealed with excitement. Brianna watched as all the dragonflies took flight around her. Their wings pushing and pulling at the air. She laughed and held on tight to Mrs. Moomoo as the dragonflies moved around them faster and faster, their clicking sounds growing louder and louder, until finally—swoosh!

20

When they were all gone, the yard was silent. The bees were not buzzing. The cicadas halted their wings and fell silent. Even the birds had stopped chirping.

Brianna's heart drummed loudly in her ears, and her chest pumped faster as she tried to catch her breath. When she opened her eyes and looked around the yard, she could not find one dragonfly. Not in the garden. Not on her sandbox. Not one dragonfly remained. *It's like magic*, Brianna thought.

"Was that magic, Mama?" Brianna whispered into the stillness.

"Yes, Brianna," her mother whispered as she swirled the magic wand in a circle above Brianna's head. "I believe that really was magic."

"We did it, Mrs. Moomoo," she said looking into the eyes of her friend. "We found magic."

CPSIA information can be obtained
at www.ICGtesting.com
Printed in the USA
BVOW05s0850120817
491886BV00005B/9/P